THE DOM'S SONGBIRD

A BILLIONAIRE ROMANCE

MICHELLE LOVE

CONTENTS

1. Chapter One — 1
2. Chapter Two — 6
3. Chapter Three — 12
4. Chapter Four — 23
5. Chapter Five — 29
6. Chapter Six — 36
7. Chapter Seven — 41
8. Chapter Eight — 48
9. Chapter nine — 57
10. Chapter Ten — 63
11. Chapter Eleven — 68

Made in "The United States" by:

Michelle Love

© Copyright 2020 – Michelle Love

ISBN: 978-1-64808-211-5

ALL RIGHTS RESERVED. No part of this publication may be reproduced or transmitted in any form whatsoever, electronic, or mechanical, including photocopying, recording, or by any informational storage or retrieval system without express written, dated and signed permission from the author

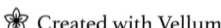 Created with Vellum

Dark and dangerous desires run wild at the exclusive seaside resort owned by Donovan Fox. He's a wealthy man with the world at his fingertips, and frankly he's bored with it all. Then he takes possession of the penthouse, and meets his own employee, Gwen Lovett, a sweet-faced aspiring singer. Then he learns that there's something about Gwen that pulls him in like a magnet, and Gwen learns that Donovan wakens something inside her that takes her breath away as much as it scares her. Can the billionaire and the songbird waitress cross the dark waters together and learn how deeply they can love?

When it comes to romance and love, Donovan Fox, powerful hotel magnate just says "no thanks." He likes his women worldly and as good at the game as he is, so when he runs into a sweet and shy waitress pressed into unexpected room service, he thinks she's adorable and not much else.

However, Gwen Love's got a voice like an angel, a spirit that rises up no matter what knocks her down, and a sensual streak that speaks to something darkly primitive in Donovan's own usually cold heart.

It becomes Donovan's sole mission to seduce the blond chanteuse into his bed, but while he isn't looking, Gwen find her way into his heart instead. Can the billionaire and the songbird find a place where their song will truly be heard?

CHAPTER ONE

Gwen

It was the sweet lull after the lunch rush had died down and the dinner rush hadn't yet to begin. We were supposed to be rolling up more silverware for the tables, but instead, Andrea and Carly and I were taking a little break in the tiny courtyard outside of the restaurant. Carly was hiding a cigarette in her hand, Andrea was fighting with her mom on Facebook, and I was just trying to recover from the press of people from lunch.

"You look like hell, hon," Carly said, glancing at me. "Did you stay up all night again?"

I grinned ruefully. "Not all night."

Andrea looked up from her phone to frown at me.

"I would feel better about that if you were actually staying up for something fun. Was it more music?"

I made a face, and Carly chuckled. "That song about the girl and the bird and the man again?"

I sighed, which was as good as saying yes. "It's coming along. I just want it to be perfect, and... it's not."

Andrea snorted. "No such thing as perfect in this world. Not when there are bills to pay. Get it good enough, and move on."

I knew that Andrea was right. People didn't make livings off of perfect songs. They wrote a lot of songs, refined their skills, sang their heads off whenever they could, and over time, if they were lucky, if they were clever and quick enough, they might make it.

I wasn't built that way, however. I wanted this song to be perfect, and despite all the evidence to the contrary, I thought maybe I could get it there. Maybe if I just put in enough work, enough time, enough long nights...

Carly interrupted my thoughts with a gentle elbow in my ribs and a nod towards the atrium. Across from the restaurant in the courtyard was the hotel lobby, where we could see jet setters from all over the world checking in. The sunny Florida beaches brought all sorts of people to the Fox Hotel, Resort and Suites, but I could tell who Carly was pointing at right away.

"Well look at that," said Andrea, impressed.

The man walking into the hotel was handsome, but then it was a high-end luxury resort. We saw handsome people every day. This man was different. He was in his late thirties or early forties with a lean body that was only emphasized by his well-cut linen suit. His dark hair was a stark contrast to the pale suit, sleeked back in a fashionable cut, and when he smiled, his white teeth flashed. For just a moment, I was convinced that he had seen us, or rather, seen me. Our eyes locked, and in the back of my mind, I noted that his eyes seemed as dark as his hair, almost sinister.

Then he half-turned to greet a gorgeous redhead in an emerald designer dress—one that looked like it would cost a year of my salary, bare minimum—and to offer his arm and a quick kiss. I stifled a sigh. Of course it was ridiculous that he had even noticed me for a moment; whoever he was, he didn't keep company with cheap little waitress.

The three of us watched as he crossed the lobby and was greeted by a dark-haired woman who looked fresh out of the pool, clad in a long and flowing robe. My eyebrows shot up to my hairline as I saw him offer her a kiss.

"Oh come on," I muttered. The man, a gorgeous woman on either arm, merely nodded at the concierge and swept towards the elevators to the penthouse suites.

"Well, that was like being visited by royalty," Carly said shaking her head, and at my confused look, she added, "That was Donovan Fox."

"The owner of the hotel?" That was an admitted surprise. I had been working at the hotel for almost two years, and had never given its owner much thought. I was too making ends meet. If it did ever cross my mind, I just assumed he was a stuffy older man with a golf habit. The man we had just seen in the lobby might have been a golfer, but that certainly wasn't the game he had in mind just now.

Andrea laughed at the slight blush on my cheeks.

"Awww, does baby girl not know that she's working for a damned Casanova?" she cooed. "That man gets more tail than all the Kennedys combined."

"Stop it, you're embarrassing her," Carly chided. "I'm surprised that you've never seen him around here before, Gwen. He shows up, usually with a beautiful woman or two on his arm, checks to make sure things are going well, and then moves on after a few weeks. He gets treated like a king, but he does tip well."

"That's good, I guess," I said dubiously, and Andrea threw an arm over my shoulders.

"Do you want to get in good with Donovan Fox, sweetie?

Maybe if you sing him a pretty song, he'll make you famous, huh?"

"Oh god, no." I pushed her away. "Like the man would give a damn about my voice."

Andrea smirked. "Fair enough. His physical appetites are legendary. So maybe your sexy throat instead ... I bet he could make you sing ..."

"Hey, we need another eighty silverware rolls before dinner!" Gus yelled from inside.

All three of us made a face at our boss' summons and we got up to file back into the restaurant.

As I went back to work, I found myself thinking again about Donovan Fox. The phrase *handsome as the devil* drifted across my mind, and the shiver that ran down my spine startled me. My mind drifted to what he was very likely doing with the two gorgeous women right now, and then I forced myself to go back to the task at hand.

I had absolutely no business with Donovan Fox. He didn't know me; he never would. End of story.

"Gus, I don't do room service, I'm a waitress!" I protested, but the restaurant manager was obviously not listening.

"And I'm not a cook, but here I am," he growled, finishing off the plates he was prepping. He might not have been a cook, but it looked good to me, sausage and eggs and toast with a small bowl of carefully cut fruit. The silver cover clanged down over all of it, and I jumped a little.

"This isn't my job," I repeated, and Gus shook his head.

"This is a special case. Just get the food up to the penthouse, and that's it. The house staff got hit by the flu, and there's no one else. Go upstairs, hand off the tray, and come back. Not difficult, so drop the tantrum already."

I scowled, but took the tray from him and stalked out.

If I were honest, I was sort of scared of room service. I had heard way too many stories of girls who got harassed by terrible male guests, and that didn't even cover some of the weird things room service workers saw. Some time last year, a room service worker had gotten bitten by an actual pet cheetah that some guest had smuggled in. I could deal with the crowds in the restaurant, but something about possibly being trapped in a room with an unpleasant guest gave me the creeps.

Just this once won't hurt, I told myself. *Get in, get out, and you're done. That's all.*

The order slip told me that I was delivering to a penthouse, and despite my anxiety, I enjoyed the swift ride to the top in the elegant wood paneled elevator. One full side was hazy glass, letting me look out over the sea close by.

The doors whooshed open at the top and there were two women waiting for the elevator as I got off of it. They were chatting companionably, well-dressed and obviously freshly-showered, and I wouldn't have given it a second thought if I hadn't recognized them. They were the redhead and the brunette from the day before, and they paid me not a single bit of attention as the elevator door closed behind me.

I swallowed hard. All right. I hadn't expected to deliver breakfast to the owner of the hotel this morning, but this didn't have to be weird. Go in, drop off, get out, and get back to my comfort zone downstairs.

There was only one door at the end of the short hallway, and summoning up my nerve, I knocked on it.

"Come in," came a rough voice, and telling myself that I would be quick, I let myself in.

2

CHAPTER TWO

Donovan

I couldn't help breathing a slight sigh of relief when Lisle and Ana kissed me goodbye.

"Did we wear you out?" Ana teased, and I grinned.

"Of course you did," I lied. "You need to give me some time to gather up my strength again."

Lisle pouted a little, kissing my other cheek.

"Don't take too long," she ordered. "My shoot is only going to keep me in Florida for another day."

I smiled, because as lovely as she was, as they both were, I didn't have any real interest in seeing either of them again.

I ushered them both to the door, and then feeling slightly at a loss, sat at the breakfast table at the window.

I should have felt at the top of the world. Hell, it certainly looked that way when I looked out the window. The penthouse rose twenty stories above the beach, and the blue waters of the gulf stretched out before me. I had taken over the hotel properties when I was in my twenties, and I had grown them to a world-spanning enterprise that catered to the rich and the powerful.

I should have been proud of that, and I was, but right now, all I felt was bored. Bored with the hotels, bored with the beautiful women I had just spent a good night with, bored with it all.

A hesitant knock on the door made me look up, frowning reflexively from the window. I only dimly remembered ordering room service, though the food had been more for the women than for myself.

"Come in."

The door opened and at first, I just saw the silver tray cover. The girl holding it wasn't tall, and she made herself look shorter still by keeping her head ducked down and her shoulders hitched up.

"Where would you like me to put this, sir?" she asked softly, and there was something about her voice that made me turn around to look at her more closely. There was a rich, controlled quality to it that seemed out of place somehow on her slight frame.

"Over here on the breakfast table, please."

She crossed the room to where I waited at the table, never meeting my eyes, and her gaze skittered over my form, taking in the loose linen pants that were the only garment I wore. I smiled a little when she lingered over my bare chest and shoulders.

She was dressed in the waitstaff's demure olive green sarong top and skirt, but it was hard to imagine her dealing with a sudden rush of guests at dinner time. She set the tray down, gently, and pulled off the cover. I didn't look at the food; instead I looked at her, examining her with a sudden curiosity.

"Um, is there anything else you need?" she asked, swallowing a little, and I smiled.

"Are you afraid of me?"

Whatever she had been expecting to hear, it wasn't that. Her eyes flew up to meet mine, and for the first time, I could clearly see her face.

She had a delicate kind of beauty with full lips and a faint and natural blush to her cheeks. Her eyes were an almost shockingly bright blue, fringed with long lashes, and it was too easy to imagine those eyes widening with sudden arousal or fluttering closed when she was kissed.

"What kind of question is that?" she exclaimed, holding up the tray cover as if it was some kind of shield.

"An honest one," I answered, lounging back in my chair. "You stepped in here as if it was the wolf's lair, and you were expecting to get eaten alive."

"I work in the restaurant," she hedged, looking away, "and we really aren't meant to be doing room service."

"Is room service work really so awful?" I asked curiously, and she flushed.

"Well, you hear things. Bad guests, every now and then a girl gets trapped in a room, that one girl got bitten by a cheetah..."

I blinked, because whatever she was going to say, I really wasn't expecting that.

"What? A cheetah? Girls getting trapped?"

She lifted one slender shoulder in a shrug. "There's a reason I'm nervous. Room service is sort of risky."

I scowled, because I certainly hadn't heard anything of the sort.

"Well, thank you for telling me about that. I'm sorry it's a terror. And I assure you that I don't bite." Even as I spoke, my mind wandered to how very supple her soft skin looked. Eminently bitable, frankly.

She must have heard something in my voice that alarmed her, because she looked suddenly worried.

"It's... not as bad as all that. Please, I really like my job..."

I rolled my eyes at how terrified she looked suddenly.

"Stop that, I'm not going to fire you for telling me the damn truth," I said, and she nodded, still looking unconvinced. I sighed, glancing at her name tag.

"Gwen, right? Gwen, I need to know when things like that are happening so I can make sure that they stop. I'm glad you told me."

She nodded, unconvinced. It was probably the best I could do, and the most merciful thing would be to send her back to the kitchen. For some reason, I didn't want to do that, however. Instead, I slouched back in my chair, looking her over.

Slender and small, she wasn't my usual type; I generally preferred my women to be curvy. Still there was something about her that drew my attention, that made me want to reach out and see if I could wipe that scared look out of her eyes.

"Do you work her full time, Gwen?"

"I do, sir."

"Call me Donovan," I commanded. "When I want you to call me sir, I'll let you know."

The blush that seemed permanent on her cheeks deepened even further, and something in me roused. I wondered for a moment what it would be like to have her calling me sir, waiting for my next order and looking at me with pleasure in her eyes instead of fear.

"Donovan," she said, as if she were trying the name out in her mouth, and there was that strange husky quality in her voice again.

"You may work full time here, but that's not what you want to do, is it?" I asked, my voice soft. "What is it you want to do, Gwen?"

She swallowed, and I couldn't help standing up, getting close to her. She smelled like apple shampoo and salt; I wondered if she'd swum in the sea in the morning.

"I want to sing," she said, and I chuckled.

"Like a siren, bringing men to their doom on the rocks..."

"I'm not a siren," she said quietly. "I always think more of birds, who sing for the joy of it."

"A songbird and not a siren. That suits you, I think..."

She started to say something, but she gasped as I brought my hand up to cup her cheek. Her wide eyes got even wider and I somehow couldn't stand staying away any longer. Cupping one hand at the small of her back, pulling her closer to me, I leaned down to kiss her. I did it slowly, giving her the chance to escape if she so chose. But she didn't.

The first touch of our lips was electric, and I knew that she felt it too. She went from being stiff and nervous to melting against me, one small hand coming up to rest against my chest. She was soft and sweet under the kiss, but when I felt her tongue come out to swipe over my lower lip, I could sense the passion in her.

"Perfect little songbird, I could make you sing," I murmured, and pulled her closer to me. She tasted like pure heaven, and I felt as if I could have kissed her forever.

Then a brisk chime broke through the sensual haze, my phone going off, and with a gasp, Gwen drew back, a wine-like redness to her lips. She looked startled and wary and needy all at once, and if she hadn't stumbled back towards the door, I would have ignored the phone and started to kiss her again.

"I... I should go back to the restaurant," she stuttered. "You should get that."

I toyed with the idea of telling her to stay right where she was, but realized that might be pushing her too hard, too fast. So I nodded, atypically going against my desires. And instincts.

"The restaurant lets you customize your outfit somewhat," I said, pointing at her drab uniform. "Put some color into that. Dull and plain doesn't suit you, little songbird."

I turned away, listening to her breath stutter. Then her light steps receded, the door clicked open, then closed, and she was gone, leaving me to deal with a morning of reviews and meetings. But something about her lingered, and I determined right there and then that I would be seeing Gwen again.

CHAPTER THREE

Gwen

When I stumbled down from the penthouse, I told myself that I wouldn't think about Donovan anymore. I wouldn't think about how I'd felt when he touched me, how he had kissed me in a way that made my knees weak, what I might have done with him if that phone hadn't rung.

I knew that Carly would say it was one more asshole guest doing what he wanted, while Andrea would speculate on whether I could get money or jewelry out of it. So I didn't tell either of them what had happened in the penthouse with Donovan Fox, but it wasn't just because I didn't want to hear what they had to say.

There was also a part of me that, for some strange reason, wanted to keep the incident to myself. It wasn't just because it was private, and it wasn't because I was ashamed. The kiss had been demanding, but not forced upon me. If I hadn't wanted it, I sensed that he would have stopped. Donovan Fox didn't strike me as a man who was interested in women who didn't find him appealing.

Instead, there had been something about that encounter that had left a strange glow in me, a flickering flame that I could only keep lit if I protected it. It warmed me as I went about my busy day, even though I knew Mr. Fox—Donovan—would leave and that kiss would be likely the one and only thing we ever shared. It was enough for me.

A FEW DAYS LATER, as I was waiting for the bus that would take me from my apartment complex to the hotel, an older man wheeled a cart of flowers down the street. They were bright splashy blooms, pinks and purples and blues, and on impulse I stopped him. He smiled when I shyly took a violet-blue bloom and tucked it behind my ear before paying for it.

"Very pretty," he told me, and I smiled.

When I got to the hotel, everyone was buzzing about the changes in room service and hospitality. Some of the management had been fired, and now there was a rule that room service was always going to be two people doing runs, never one.

I flashed back to the conversation I had had with Donovan. Had he confronted management with the cheetah story? Maybe my random encounter with Donovan had done some good after all.

I mostly managed to avoid thinking of him. Several waiters had come down with the flu that the house staff had spread, so I was too busy to do more than tend to customers, especially when there was unexpected rush after a furiously powerful squall hit the beach. Heading into the dining room with more menus and a bright smile, to compensate for customers who were irate at having their beach day truncated,

I froze when I saw the man who had also come in with the rain.

Donovan lounged alone at a table, a sprinkle of water darkening his pale blue silk shirt. He gazed at me as I approached him. It was my job, after all. Nevertheless, it felt like I was somehow being pulled into his trajectory as his dark eyes watched me.

"You took my advice," he observed when I arrived at his table, and my hand came up to touch the flower nervously.

"Andrea and Carly said that it was cute," I said shyly. "I was afraid it made me look like a twelve year old..."

"Andrea and Carly are right, and no, you look nothing at all like a child."

His eyes roamed up and down my figure as if we were perfectly alone, and I clutched the menus a little closer, swallowing hard.

"I should tell you about the specials," I said softly, and he nodded, a slight amused smile on his face.

"You should," he said, and I felt as if a spell had been broken.

After he ordered, I scuttled back to the kitchen. All I could think of were the two women who had been leaving his room when we'd first met, how glamorous and beautiful they had been. It sent a strange pang of envy through me, and a self-pity that I shook off with a hard scowl.

What the heck was I even thinking?

Marshaling my mood, I moved through the dining room, taking other orders, commiserating with unhappy beachgoers, and bringing out the food as fast as the overwhelmed kitchen staff could come up with it. I didn't have time to dawdle, and Donovan's courtesy surprised me. After our initial interaction, he didn't try to distract me further. I brought him his meal, he thanked me, and I hurried away, still feeling his eyes on me.

I didn't even realize what he had done until it was time to

cash out. Chuy's eyes widened when he was totaling up my tips, and then I gasped when he handed me what must have been more than 300 dollars, more than half from Donovan, and I swallowed hard. Everyone in the hotel talked about how generous he was, but I had the feeling that there was something more to this. A mixture of excitement and worry filled me. A man so wealthy could easily be implying he was buying me, had it not been for his impeccable manners thus far. Even the kiss—the.kiss.—he'd given me ample space to make a decision about whether or not I'd wanted it. And I had. So very badly.

Just as I was headed for my locker, Gus stopped me.

"Delivery to the penthouse," he said, pointing at a cart, and I frowned.

"Aren't we supposed to be going in pairs now?"

"That's for official room service, and you aren't. Quick run, in and out, and then you can head home."

I wasn't surprised at all when I saw on the order ticket that it was Donovan's penthouse suite, and as I went up the elevator, I felt a dozen butterflies in my stomach. I took a deep breath, and at his crisp "come in," I ventured into the room warily.

"Is your last name really Love?" he asked as soon as I entered his apartment.

He was sprawled on the leather couch in the sunken living room, his shirt unbuttoned halfway down his muscled chest, watching me with hungry curiosity that made me think less of cheetahs than it did a lion lying in wait.

"It is," I said, proud of the fact that my voice didn't shake at all. "Believe me, I've heard all of the jokes, so unless you think you have a new one..."

The answer popped out of my mouth before I could stop it, and I swallowed a startled groan. Since when did I run my mouth with anybody, much less the man who paid my salary?

But instead of being irritated, Donovan laughed.

"No, all of the ones that I could think of were terrible, so I let it go. You wear it well?"

"The flower?"

"No, the name. It suits you."

"If you say so," I said dubiously. "Where would you like the food?"

"On the coffee table is fine. Are you hungry?"

I shook my head as I set down his tray of cheese, fruit and sliced sausage. Then my stomach rumbled, and Donovan laughed.

"Liar ... Your shift is over. Come sit here with me and have some of this."

I hadn't eaten since noon, but refusing him anything wasn't something I thought would be easy.

"That's really not something we're meant to do with a guest."

Wordlessly, Donovan passed me a slice of pale cheese on a dark cracker and I sank down on the far end of the couch, crunching into it gratefully when Donovan spoke again, his eyes trailing over me lazily.

"Do you have a boyfriend, Gwen?"

I bit my tongue sharply, just barely managed to avoid spitting out the cracker, and stared at him.

"What kind of question is that?"

Donovan chuckled. "An honest one that deserves an honest answer, I think."

I wasn't so sure about that.

"Well, no, I don't have a boyfriend...Why do you want to know?"

For a moment, he just looked at me as if wondering what planet I came from.

"Are you serious?" he asked. "You have no idea why a man might ask an attractive woman if she's seeing anyone? None at all?"

"I'm not an attractive woman," I said bluntly, "and I saw the two women who left this penthouse a few days ago. So yeah, I guess I don't have a clue."

He grinned a little at my tone, and I scowled at him. I was beginning to be less worried about losing my job if I said the wrong thing, and more frustrated with Donovan for thinking he got to ask whatever questions he wanted.

"You're wrong," Donovan offered. "I think you're quite attractive, and if that kiss we shared the last time you were here is any indication, you think the same about me. And while you didn't seem to be the sort to kiss when you had a boyfriend at home, I wasn't sure."

I gritted my teeth and reached for another slice of cheese. If i had to deal with him thinking I was some kind of cheater, I could damn well be fed for the privilege.

"That's flattering," I muttered, and he laughed again. I had to admit I enjoyed the low, husky sound.

"Well, a lot of the women that I deal with don't really mind stepping out on their lovers that much."

"Then you need to hang out with different women," I retorted.

"You're probably not wrong. So far, it seems to be going pretty well for me. What about for you?" he teased.

"The food is good," I admitted grudgingly.

"What about the kiss?"

Once again, I nearly choked on a cracker. "It was ... nice," I mumbled.

"Oh, songbird," he murmured, shaking his head. "You're lying to me again. I think we both know it was a whole lot more than that."

I dodged that line of conversation. "I heard what you did for room service. Thank you."

Donovan nodded, a faint shadow stealing over his face.

"That was a bad business that should have been stopped long before now."

"I noticed that it doesn't apply to waitstaff, though," I said, and there was a sudden gleam in his eyes, one that made my heart beat a little faster.

"Well, waitstaff shouldn't be making runs to guests' rooms at all."

"And yet, here I am."

"Yes."

He leaned in, eyes locked on mine. I could have stopped him. I could have stood up and told him I was done and that I was going home. No matter what caution told me, there was a voice at the back of my head that said he wouldn't fire me for it.

I didn't.

Instead, I leaned into the hand that came up to cradle the side of my face, and when he kissed me, I parted my lips for him.

The last kiss had been fast, like a lion pouncing on its prey. This one... I felt seduced, as if somehow the lion, with its golden beauty and it's basso profundo rumble, had convinced me it was tame.

I felt a thrilling shock of electricity run through me as he kissed me, and I leaned in, wanting more. I had kissed men before, of course, boyfriends, dares, that sort of thing. The difference in kissing them and kissing Donovan was as wide as the ocean.

I could feel the teeth in his kiss, and it left my mouth feeling sensuously tender and soft. He wasn't content kissing my mouth, however, and I gasped a little as he tilted my head to one side, nuzzling against my jaw before dropping a line of kisses along my throat.

"I can't," I found myself whispering. "I can't..."

He paused and pulled back long enough to look at me. Donovan on his own was handsome enough, but Donovan aroused, with that gleaming light in his eyes and his mouth reddened from our kiss, was utterly devastating.

"Why?" he asked reasonably, and his tone was so kind that I couldn't help throwing my arms around him and pressing my face to his chest. After a startled moment, he wrapped me in his arms.

"Did someone hurt you before?" he asked, a silky thread of menace in his voice. It took me a moment before I realized what he was asking.

"What... no! No, not at all. It's just..."

"Just..."

"I'm not... this type of girl," I said weakly. There was a heat centered low in my belly and an electric tingle that danced over my skin that demurred, but I shook my head.

"What kind of girl are you, then?" he asked, and I laughed a little.

"One that definitely does not belong in a penthouse, kissing her boss," I said, and he made a sound that was suspiciously similar to a purr.

"If I'm your boss, doesn't that mean that I get to tell you what to do?"

"I..."

"Maybe I say that you belong right here." His voice dropped and I could feel his lips moving next to my ear right before he nipped at my earlobe. The sharp prick of pain startled me, making me yelp, and then he was kissing that sharpness away, lapping at my earlobe with a clever tongue.

I wanted to reply, but what he was doing with his mouth took my breath away, making me cling closer to him.

"Maybe I say that you belong next to me, underneath me, letting me touch you and make you feel good. And believe me, Gwen, I can make you feel so good. I want to lie you down and touch you, show you exactly what that beautiful little body was made for."

I whimpered a little as he pressed me back against the couch, looming over me to kiss a path down my jaw. His dexterous fingers found the knots that held the sarong top of my uniform closed at the shoulders, undoing one and kissing the bare skin it revealed there.

"You taste good," Donovan murmured to me. "Did you know that? Like salt and honey and sweetness. How in the world has no one eaten you up yet?"

I tried to garble out some kind of reply, but then he was swiping his tongue along my collarbone, finding all sorts of sensitive spots that I didn't know I had. One hand was on my shoulder, steadying me, and the other stroked my knee through the thin skirt. I wanted his skin on my bare skin, but for the moment, he seemed content to take his time, driving me slowly crazy with the pleasure he was offering.

"If I'm you're boss, and you have to do what I say, maybe you would like taking orders, hm?" he asked, and I couldn't stop from shivering underneath him. "What if I ordered you to strip yourself bare for me?"

"Why?" I squeaked out, and instead of laughing at me, he only leaned up to kiss me again. This man could take my breath away with his kisses, and when he pulled back again, there was humor in his eyes, but also something wild and needy as well.

"Because I want to see you," Donovan growled, his voice hoarse. "Because you are so beautiful, and I want to see it all bare for me. I would make you turn around so I could see all of you, and I would make you march right back to the bedroom, wait for me flat on your back, your arms and legs out because only I could touch you..."

Desire ran through me like someone had suddenly undammed a river, and it nearly made me dizzy. With just his words, I could imagine him doing all of that to me with crystal clarity. It didn't shock me, exactly. What shocked me was how very much I wanted him to do it. I had always thought that I was something of a cold fish when it came to romance, but apparently what it had taken was this man and his words, unraveling me like a scarf until I had come completely undone...

It was too much, and with a cry, I squirmed away from him and lurched to my feet. For a moment, he stared after me as if all he wanted was to drag me back. Then a rueful look came over his face.

"No?" he asked, and no matter how panicked I was or shocked that I had been so open to what he was talking about, I couldn't bring myself to tell him no.

"I... I need to go," I said, the words stumbling out of my mouth. "I should... go..."

"If you want to," he said quietly. "But really, there was another reason I asked you here."

I blinked. "There... was?"

"I looked you up on online. I found some of the recordings you've made."

Whatever I had been expecting, that wasn't it. I had made those recordings at home with a borrowed microphone, facing a corner of my little apartment that had been draped with blankets to improve the sound quality. I had been proud at the time, but in short order had seen how amateurish they were compared to what other people were producing.

"You're good," he said, "and I'd like to hire you. Come sing here on Friday night. I'm meeting with some people from the hotels in the area. I think you have a good voice, and I'd like you to sing that night."

"I... I don't have anything to wear to anything so fancy," I blurted out, and then I shook my head. "I've never sung in front of an audience before."

"First time for everything."

Donovan reached into his wallet, and peeled away what looked like three hundred dollars, stuffing it into my hand.

"There you go, dress fee paid, and it'll be another three hundred at the end of the performance. If you are taking requests, I'm partial to blue on you."

"You're serious," I said slowly. "You want me to come sing for you."

"I am always serious, songbird," he said, and though his gaze was soft, I could still see that predatory gleam there. "Friday night. Show up at ten. I'll be expecting you."

CHAPTER FOUR

Donovan

Getting a group of independent millionaires to agree to anything was like herding cats. By the time dinner was over, I was ready to be done with it all.

I had poured myself a couple fingers of Scotch when there was a shy knock on the door. Knowing who it was already, I didn't stop the smile that crossed my face as I walked over to open the door, then stopped as Gwen was revealed before me in all her soft, delicate beauty, this time enrobed in a sapphire dress.

The dress fell almost to the ground, even with the tall heels she wore so nervously. I could see the weight of it as she walked shyly into the room, casting a nervously hopeful look at me. While the dress covered her completely from hip to ground, it was cut low enough to show off her slight curves on top, leaving her shoulders nearly bare except for a pair of slender jeweled straps. There were a pair of bright glittery rhinestone barrettes in her hair, completing the picture. She looked like some perfect mix of innocent and sultry, right down to the pink lipstick that had been applied so artfully. Whoever this Andrea was, she probably deserved a raise.

"Is it all right?" Gwen asked softly, and I reached out to stroke her cheek.

"You look stunning."

"I wanted to look nice. For your guests. For you. I wouldn't want to embarrass you in any way."

I laughed softly, leaning down to brush her full lips with my own, deliberately keeping the touch light, or I knew we'd never leave the apartment. "You could never embarrass me."

"You've never heard me sing live," she whispered into the kiss and I shrugged as I forced myself to step away.

"You seem like a good bet."

It looked like she wanted to say something else, but she shook her head.

"Where do you want me?" she asked. "Should I be singing something soft when people come in, or ..."

I was suddenly tempted to see if I could make her stand on the table. That vision appealed to me, seeing her up for display, the beauty that was so easy to overlook in normal life shining like a Christmas tree. Would she like it? Would she be terrified? How easy it would be then to run my hand up her slender calf, making her shiver before moving it higher...

"Why don't you get go stand over there?" I said instead. "With your back to the window. I think that would be striking."

She moved obediently, only giving me a curious glance when I reclined on the couch not so far away.

"Should I..."

"Start with something soft," I suggested. "Give yourself time to work up to something impressive."

She smiled at me and nodded. I watched, fascinated, as her eyes fluttered closed and she seemed to compose herself.

Then Gwen started to sing and a chill ran up my spine. Her voice was lower than I would have thought, and there was something perfect and true about it. She pulled the notes effortlessly out of the air, and when she sang about a love that would never die and the abandonment of a lover, I could feel something in me that felt as if it had been asleep all my life stir.

She believes it, I realized. Her skill was impressive, her natural talent even more so, and as she stood with her back to the wide dark gulf, I could feel the heartbreak of the song running through her as well.

God, what must a full performance must be like if she felt the sweetness and the sorrow of her own songs every night?

I listened, rapt, as the song finished, and then another one started. This one was just as soft, but there was a kind of joy to it. Her eyes opened, blue as the summer sea, and I drew my breath as she started singing to me, or so it felt. When she talked about how good it felt to love and be loved, I smiled, and I could find no shade of sorrow in her at all.

As the song ended, her eyes slowly lost some of their happiness and I felt a brief kick of regret for being my usual asshole self.

"There's no one coming, is there?" she said quietly.

I shook my head. "My meeting was earlier at a very forgettable restaurant. It would have been much more entertaining if you had actually been there, singing for me."

A number of emotions chased each other over her face, anger, frustration, sorrow, a kind of wild speculation, and then she hid them away again, her face pale and neutral in a way that made me ache.

"Then what did you hire me for?"

Because I can't look away from you.

"I hired you to sing for me."

"Is that all?" she asked with such nervousness that I laughed slightly.

"Beautiful little songbird, believe me when I say that I don't need to buy my company."

Gwen's eyes narrowed and I was relieved to see some life in them again. "I was excited about my first live performance, Donovan. I practiced for days. I thought you really believed I was good enough to—"

"Stop," I warned, getting to my feet but not approaching her. "I lied only because I was uninterested in sharing you with anyone. Not because you're not talented, Gwen. You are, exceedingly. I could tell from the videos, and just now, you've blown me away."

There was still a hint of hurt in her eyes that I was suddenly desperate to erase.

"Sing for me again," I urged. "Not because I'm buying you, Gwen. But because I want to stand hear and listen to you. I *need* to."

If she'd refused me, I don't know what I would have done, but then she took a slow breath and began once more.

I lost myself in her voice. In her. In the way she didn't spare herself when she performed. When she felt an emotion from a song, she wore it as beautifully as the sapphire dress, turning from sweetness to joy to grief and back again. Her whole being seemed to vibrate as her powerful voice grew stronger with each song, filling the apartment. Filling me.

Finally, she stopped and reached for a glass of water I had placed within her reach. There was a spark of defiance in her beautiful eyes.

"Well?" she asked. "Is that what you wanted?"

"No," I admitted, though in other circumstances I would have wanted to hear her sing until the world ended. "Your singing belongs on the world's stage, but that's not all I want from you."

I watched her to see if she would gather herself up and walk out. Instead, she wavered, glancing at the door, glancing at me. Her obvious uncertainty moved me in ways very little ever did.

"Come here," I said softly, and was relieved when she slowly crossed the floor to stand in front of me. I looked her up and down, something that brought that lovely color to her cheeks again, and smiled down into her eyes.

"There is absolutely no flaw in you," I told her. "I could stand here forever and listen. I could stand here forever and look."

"I'm not–"

"No." My sharp command visibly startled her to stillness.

"You're not going to contradict me on something I know to be true. There are consequences for that."

She licked her lips, and I managed to hold myself back. Soon.

"And what are those consequences?" she asked, her voice soft and husky. Did she even know how beautiful she looked?

"Whatever I think suits the crime," I said easily. "Maybe a spanking. Maybe I'll take that dress right off of you and drive you home in your underwear."

She shuddered, and at first I thought she was thinking of having all of her delectable charms exposed, but then she looked at me, her blue eyes wide and wanting.

"Don't make me leave," she said, her voice aching, and any resolve that I had to draw this out shattered.

I took her hand and dragged her into me, kissing her roughly. She whimpered a little when my teeth pressed against her soft lip, but still clung to me with all of her strength.

"I want you," I told her between kisses. "I've wanted you ever since the first time I saw you. If you want to leave, do it now, because otherwise, I'm not letting you out of bed until morning."

She didn't pause at all. Instead Gwen pressed herself even closer to me, her kisses shy but hungry.

"Please," she said, and as I pulled her close to me, I wondered if I was ever going to be able to let her go.

CHAPTER FIVE

Gwen

I knew that there were words for singers who slept with their clients. None of them were kind, and all of them could end a career before it even got off of the ground. However, all that mattered to me right now was Donovan's hot mouth on mine, his strong and solid body underneath me.

When he stood, cradling me against his chest, I gasped at the shift of his powerful muscles banded around my body.

"You feel perfect in my arms," Donovan murmured. "Exactly as I've imagined, and I've been imagining a lot, Gwen."

I blushed and he kissed me hard as he carried me to the bedroom. It was dominated by a king-sized bed that seemed to stretch from wall to wall, and when he laid me down on it, I sighed in surprised pleasure. It was pure luxury lying on the bed and watching him move around the edges of it.

"Your breath caught when I talked about making you walk outside naked," he said, almost casually, and I gulped.

"That would be embarrassing, wouldn't it?" I asked, and he gave me an amused look.

"Is that all it would be?"

I knew he was looking as I pressed my legs together more tightly, squirming a little.

"No," I admitted, and Donovan laughed.

"I think we are going to have a fine time together tonight," he said, reaching for my hand.

I gave it to him without thinking, and then blinked when he tied a silk tie around my wrist.

"Donovan!"

"Do you trust me?" he asked. I sighed, because he was stroking the skin of my palm with a gentle finger.

"Yes ... I think."

"Good. Everything we do tonight, it's all for making you feel good, all right? If you don't like anything, speak up... but I think you will."

He waited until I nodded to lash the other end of the tie to the headboard. My other hand received the same treatment, and in a matter of seconds, I was pinioned to the mattress, my arms stretched up over my head. Donovan stopped to look at me for a moment, and I whimpered a little at how heated his glance was.

"Perfect. Just perfect."

I opened my mouth to tell him that he was obviously mistaken, but predatory look in his eyes made me shut my mouth. I wondered if he would really make good on his threat to make me walk out the door without my dress on, but I realized that even if he wouldn't do that, he would absolutely give me a spanking...

"Good girl," he chuckled, as if reading my thoughts. "Now let's see about that dress..."

The bed dipped under his weight as he came to kneel between my legs. He moved forward until I had to spread my legs wide, and even if my dress still covered me, I could feel how very exposed I was to him, to his eyes, his hands.

There was a zipper along the back of the dress, but Donovan didn't even bother with it. Instead, he took took each jeweled strap in his hands and broke it before ripping my dress right down the front. I gasped at both the heavy ripping sound and the sudden exposure. My brain was shocked at the destruction of such an expensive dress, but then I was far more concerned about suddenly being in my underwear in front of Donovan.

"God, so very beautiful," he purred, dropping a kiss just below my collarbones. "So very perfect..."

This time, I couldn't muster a reply because his weight over me, his mouth on me, were all too much. It just all felt so good, and I wanted to get my hands all over him, but I couldn't.

"I've thought about you like this, all perfectly open for me," Donovan muttered. "I'm going to make you feel so good, songbird."

I started to say something, and then I could only moan as he worked his way down my body, pausing to stroke my breasts with just the gentlest touch of his fingertips. I had never thought my breasts were so sensitive before, but his light touch made me ache for me, arching towards him. When he set one mouth to my nipple, I couldn't stop myself from whimpering out loud as he licked it until it was standing proudly.

"So perfect," Donovan muttered, and maybe I should have been embarrassed about how intimately he was speaking, but instead I felt a strange pride in how much he wanted me.

Donovan kissed his way down my belly, making me giggle a little, and then he smiled at the lacy dark panties I wore. I thought he would tear them off just as he had torn off my dress, but instead he lifted my legs up and eased the scrap of lace down my legs instead. He kissed my thigh before laying them back down, and something about the tenderness there made me sigh.

"Now I want to look at you," Donovan purred, and I gasped as he spread my legs wide.

I had never been looked as so thoroughly by a lover before. Donovan handled me as if I were something sacred and precious, and before he leaned down to place a gentle kiss on my soft mound, I was already squirming for him.

He stretched out on the bed as if we had all the time in the world, kissing my soft inner thighs and the crease where my legs met my body. Teasingly, he brushed the very tip of his tongue along my slit, making me shiver a little. When he circled my clit with just the ball of his thumb, I made a little longing noise, and he obligingly pressed his fingers against me a little more firmly.

"Look at how wet you are getting, beautiful girl," he murmured. "So wet and perfect for me..."

He pressed one finger inside me as he lapped at my clit, making me buck up against his touch. God I wanted to touch him then. I wanted to bury my hands in that sleek dark hair, not to try to get more of that delicious sensation but to simply be closer to him. Instead, I was pinned and helpless to do anything besides lie there and take the pleasure he was offering me.

Soon enough, he was pressing two fingers inside me and then three. Instead of flinching away, I had my heels dug into the mattress, pushing up against him as best i could. I wanted him so badly that I was uttering his name in soft gasps, pleading little sounds that made him groan.

"God, but you're irresistible," he said, rising up and wiping his mouth with the back of his hand. "I wanted to stretch this out, wanted you to beg me for your release but I don't think I can..."

There was something intoxicating about knowing that i had seduced him even when I was utterly helpless.

"I want you," I managed to whimper. "Please. Don't resist... just give me... please give me..."

I stuttered to a stop because I wasn't sure if i could say it, and he grinned at me briefly.

"Another time," he promised. "Another time, I'll lay you down and make you spell out exactly what it is you want me to do. I won't care if it takes all day. I'll make you say it.

"But not today."

I had just a moment to be relieved that he wasn't going to be that cruel, but then he pulled away, reaching for something in the nightstand close by. For the first time since he had tied me to the bed, I wasn't touching him in any way and the sudden cold made me panic.

I must have made a gasping noise because he was right back in a moment, kissing me and stroking my hair out of my face.

"Don't worry, pretty one, I'm not going to leave you here like this. I would never..."

I relaxed into his touch and his words, and then I watched as he drew his cock out of his pants. He laughed when he caught me licking my lips, but I refused to be embarrassed by it. He was thick and hard, and there was something ridiculously hot about the way he smoothed the latex down, sheathing all of that primal hardness.

"Are you ready, beautiful?" he asked, and I nodded hard, unable to speak.

I thought that he would untie me then but instead he only touched my hands gently before going down to kneel between my thighs.

"Mine," he murmured, and there was a powerfully possessive note in his voice, something was more than what he had said before. There was almost a kind of wonder in his voice as he pressed the very tip of his cock against my entrance.

As he sank into me, I sighed with pleasure my eyes fluttering shut. He filled me perfectly, and for a moment, we were utterly still. Then he started to move, and the pleasure only rose higher and higher inside me.

"So good," he growled, his voice rough with passion. "You feel so perfect..."

I didn't have words any longer. Instead, all I had were the soft noises he was forcing out of me. I writhed underneath him. All I wanted at that point was to have more of him. I would have sold my soul to touch him, to reach for him.

Instead, all I could do was take the pleasure that was rising in waves through my body. drawing tighter and tighter like a thin silver wire... until it snapped.

"Donovan!" I cried, and the climax took me apart. Something about being tied down, unable to move or reach for him, made my climax all the more powerful, and I sobbed helplessly as it ripped through me.

"Beautiful girl," Donovan muttered, leaning down to kiss my throat. "So beautiful..."

I was still recovering from the force of my pleasure as he thrust into me one last time. I felt his thrusts become more powerful, more erratic, and then finally he thrust into me one last time, freezing for a moment. Then, as I watched, he came apart just as I had, melting into me.

I knew he was wearing a condom, but for just a moment, I imagined what it would be like if he weren't, if I could feel him claiming me in one of the most absolute ways possible.

He rested his weight on me for a moment, and then he rolled to one side. For a moment, I was panicked that he might leave me again, but instead he watched me, one hand stretched casually over my belly as if we did this all the time.

"Tell me something?" he asked, his voice hoarse.

"Of course."

"If I could give you anything you wanted right now, what would it be?"

"Easy," I said with a smile. I would want you to untie me so I could touch you."

The sound he made was pure masculine pleasure, and he reached up to undo the ties that had held me captive. To my surprise, he held my hands in his for a moment, kissing each finger before looking up at me.

"All right? No numbness or anything like that?"

"No, not at all."

"Good. I don't want to hurt you, Gwen. I never want that."

I didn't want to think about hurting or anything like that at the moment. Right then, all I wanted was to be close to him, and newly freed, I could do that. I pressed myself close to his body, burying my face in his chest, and I sighed with pleasure.

"This was what I wanted," I said, suddenly drowsy, and I heard him laugh.

CHAPTER SIX

Donovan

I kept my promise to Gwen. We explored each other thoroughly that night, and we both fell asleep some time not long before dawn. When I woke up, sunlight was streaming in through the window, warm and sweet, and I realized something odd.

I had a good time with women, and I liked to think that they had a good time with me. That good time was usually something with an expiration date, however. We enjoyed each other's company and then we left one another in the morning, moving on with our respective lives. As I glanced at Gwen, sleeping curled on her side with a spray of golden hair in her face, I realized I didn't want her to leave.

I hadn't had a woman in my bed like her in a long while, one that wanted me to lead and then rewarded me with a pure and gorgeously perfect response. That was what I told myself. Somewhere deep inside me, however, I knew that it was far more than that. I had never before had anyone like Gwen at all, never run into her passion, her delicate sweetness, her intoxicating combination of innocence and sensuality.

I didn't want to lose it yet.

In the dining room, I made a few calls, and by the time that was done, I could hear her stirring in the bedroom. I got back to her just in time to see her examining the dress that I had torn off of her.

"I need to figure out what I'm going to wear when I'm get home."

"That's nothing to worry about," I said with a shrug, although the thought of her leaving made me suddenly tense. "For now, just put on one of my shirts. Food will be here in a few minutes."

Despite her worry about her clothes, Gwen brightened at the mention of food, and I was glad that I had told room service to bring up a little of everything.

"Go shower," I told her. "Food will be here when you're done."

While the water was running, I thought about what it would be like to come in after her, to step behind her in all of that hot steaming water. Would she let me wash her? Would she let me touch her in all the intimate spots that I was coming to know so well. I imagined her bent over the bathroom sink as I took her from behind, and it was all I could do to stay where I was, waiting for the food.

She came out dressed in one of my dress shirts and not ravaging her right then and there took almost all the restraint I had left in me.

We were quiet dining companions at first, but apparently food was what it took to loosen her tongue.

"This all looks so good, and I don't even recognize half of the fruit here... What's that one?"

"Dragon fruit," I said with a smile. "Try it, it's nice and sweet..."

Whenever she tasted something new, she insisted I try it as well, and though I laughed, I could feel something inside me coming unmoored, untethered. I loved indulging my partners in bed, but that was usually as far as it went. In its own way, sharing food with Gwen, letting her feed me what was on her plate, was almost as intimate as what we had done the night before.

All too soon, though, breakfast was over, and Gwen sighed.

"I guess I need to start thinking about how to get home," she said. "I'm off for the weekend, but I know you're busy."

Before I could say anything, there was another knock on the door. Gwen froze, unsure of what to do, but I smiled at her.

"Don't worry. I'm expecting them. Stay right there."

I came back with a double armful of bags, setting them on the couch.

"Here, these are for you."

She blinked, walking over to look through the bags in shock. I saw her face register delight and confusion, and finally she turned to me.

"There must be at least a thousand dollars' worth of clothing in here...."

"I didn't know what you wanted or liked, so I asked my personal shopper to make some decisions."

"But how did you..."

I held up the tag that I had cut off of her ruined gown. It had her size on it, but Gwen still looked confused.

"This is too much," she said, and I grinned.

"Not if you're coming to Atlanta with me."

She looked at me as if I had gone insane, and I laughed again. There was something about surprising her that delighted me.

"What's in Atlanta?"

"Some kind of museum opening. It's marked on my calendar as something I should absolutely not miss, and I wouldn't mind having a pretty date on my arm. If you say yes, I can make arrangements for suitable attire there, but these clothes should be perfect for seeing the town."

"Well, they're perfect if there were five of me," she said absently, and then Gwen raised those extraordinary blue eyes to me.

"What is this?" she asked softly.

I frowned.

"What do you mean?"

"Well, we had... an unforgettable night, one that... well, unforgettable. And amazing. But now you're buying me clothing and taking me away for the weekend..."

"Is that not what people do when they like each other?" I asked, but I thought I saw where she was going.

"It's the kind of thing that people do when their relationship is a little more transactional than I would prefer. I know that you said you don't pay your women..."

"This isn't a payment," I said. I could feel the tension in my voice, and she winced a little.

"It feels a little like one," she said lifting her hands helplessly. "You must know that there is no way that I can give you anything half so impressive."

"You want to give me presents?" I asked in surprise, and she gave me a strangely uncomfortable look, one that was mingled disbelief and perhaps even pity. It made my hackles rise even as it made something in me, something I didn't want to look at, prowl a little closer.

"Of course I do," she said. There was that red blush on her cheeks again, but she forged forward. "We... we shared something I thought was very special. Maybe you don't think it is. Maybe I'm just making a fool of myself. But yes, I do want to give you something nice."

She looked as if she was on the verge of tears, and that overrode everything else that was making me so cautious. I crossed the space between us with just a few strides, coming to take her in my arms. She smelled like my shampoo and my laundry detergent, but underneath that was her own smell, something lovely and sweet, almost like honey and milk.

"Stop worrying about this right now," I said softly. "There is nothing transactional about this at all. I want you with me. I want you to be happy when you are, and that involves buying you some clothes, maybe taking you to a party, having some fun. This isn't... some kind of dark arrangement where I expect you to do exactly as I say for some damn clothes, Gwen."

She sighed, pressing her face against my chest.

"Promise?" she asked, and the slight tremor in her voice could have ripped my cold black heart to shreds. What was it about this beautiful young woman ...

"I do."

"And will you let me buy you a gift in Atlanta?"

I had everything that I ever wanted, and if I didn't, then I could probably have it delivered to me within twenty-four hours. But the look in her eyes, and the fact that no one who didn't have a financial stake had ever offered me gifts, combined in my mind as I murmured, "Yes."

CHAPTER SEVEN

Gwen

Atlanta had a graceful and almost melancholic elegance to it. Where I was from in Florida, everything was new and oftentimes ugly as well. Atlanta seemed to hang on to whatever beauty it could lay hands on, no matter how old. When I mentioned this to Donovan, he smiled a little.

"I've always liked Atlanta for precisely that reason," he said. "Florida might be more fun, but Georgia has deep, deep roots."

He had flown us into a private airstrip, my first experience with a private jet, and when we touched down in Georgia, there was a sleek dark car waiting for us.

"Are we staying at another hotel?" I asked, and he smiled.

"I thought about it, but I have some property here I think you might like."

The small house on the very outskirts of Atlanta's most fashionable neighborhood was gorgeous, surrounded by a tall fence covered with creeping myrtle, and though it had all the modern accouterments, it was clear that the form of it had stood the test of time.

"Good bones," Donovan said as I looked around at all the polished wood and glass. "I bought this house years ago when I was thinking about doing more business in Atlanta. I don't know if I've stayed more than a total of a month or so in it, though."

"If I owned this place, I don't know if I would ever leave," I murmured, looking out the back window into the lush garden in the back."

"Well, let's see if you still think that when you see my place in LA," Donovan said with a laugh.

He had talked about the future a few times in the plane, talked about taking me traveling to see what other beautiful cities he had business in. It made me feel warm inside, but there was still that wariness at the heart of it, the question of what we were to each other, and what this could all mean.

"Your dress is upstairs in the master bedroom," he said with a smile. "You should go see if it suits you."

Donovan followed me as I went up the stairs, and when I saw the dress that had been laid out for me on the enormous bed, I gasped a little.

It was a long gown in cream satin with black highlights. I could tell at a glance that it would fit me well, but there was something almost painfully sharp, painfully expensive about it.

"I can't," I said, turning to Donovan. "It's too much."

He stepped up to me, cupping the back of my neck and leaning down to kiss me.

"Of course it isn't. You need to look good for my friends, don't you?"

I did, and moreover, I knew that nothing that I could afford on my own would fit the bill. I felt as if I should protest the Cinderella treatment, but it was all too easy, far too easy to let

Donovan kiss me, hold me, lavish me with things that delighted him—and me.

It occurred to me as he showered and I got dressed that he might not know how else to show he liked someone. He wanted to give me gifts, get me things that I couldn't have on my own, and my pleasure in them was his pleasure as well. I wondered with a pang if he had ever experienced another kind of affection.

While we'd toured Atlanta during the day, I'd looked for something to give to him, everything I could find was too cheap, too silly, too tacky. With everything that I picked up, I was frustrated because if he wanted it, he could have picked it up before now.

Still, though, I had an idea at the back of my mind, and I thought it would work. I was jotting down a few things on a scrap of paper when he emerged from the bathroom in a cloud of steam.

"What's all that?" he asked, and I was taken all over again by how handsome he was, a dark towel draped low over his hips and his hair curling from the dampness.

"Nothing important right now," I said. "We should hurry. If you said that the museum gala starts at eight, we should leave soon."

He nodded, and with a smile pulled me into his arms for a hug. I yelped with surprise, starting to protest the rough treatment of the dress he had given me, but then the magic of his body, of the chemistry we shared between us, worked again. By the time he pulled back, I knew I would need to fix my makeup and straighten my clothes, but i still would have let him do that and more besides.

"You can't go out looking like that," he said, looking at my pink cheeks and reddened lips with amusement. "You need to get decent, songbird."

I groaned and reached for my makeup again, and when he

turned away to take care of his own clothing, I knew that he was smiling.

THE MUSEUM GALA turned out to be far more impressive than Donovan had let on. The entire museum was lit up in bright lights, there was an actual red carpet, and there were local reporters held back with just a velvet rope.

"Oh, I don't think i can do this," I murmured, and to my surprise, Donovan reached over to squeeze my hand. The smile on his face was far more gentle than I had ever seen it, and he raised my hand to his lips for a nearly courtly kiss.

"You're going to be fine, songbird. As a matter of fact, you're going to be amazing."

I took several deep breaths and managed to I exit the car without tripping or falling. Donovan offered me his arm and ushered me down the carpet and I smiled at the cameras, feeling like I was in some kind of fairytale.

"I feel like everyone is looking at me," I murmured.

"Of course they are," Donovan said, equally softly. "They've never seen a woman as beautiful as you."

At the very least, his words had the effect of making me laugh a little

"Now I know you're joking," I told him, straightening up a little.

"I don't like it when you contradict me about such things," Donovan warned, pulling me a little closer. "Come on, let's make the rounds, and you'll see."

I wasn't sure what Donovan meant for me to see. I was far too focused on smiling at the people he introduced me to, trying to make a good impression, trying not to embarrass myself and Donovan, that I barely had the energy for anything else. It was too obvious to me that these were people who I served at the Fox most of the time. They had been born to money, or had married into it. Maybe they'd even earned it. But amidst the luxury and wealth in the beautiful museum hall. I felt like a disguised intruder. At least Donovan had made sure that the disguise was a good one, but I couldn't relax, couldn't let my guard down for one moment.

The worst moment was when Donovan drifted off to talk with an acquaintance and I was left to my own devices. I felt like a moving target in the hall, and decided that the wide outdoor plaza was the safest place to be. I was just breathing in the humid fresh air with relief when there was a light touch at my elbow. I jumped and turned around to see a tall and willowy brunette with sparkling dark eyes and chestnut hair swept back in a bun offering me a glass of water.

"I saw you in there. You looked a little green around the gills when you left," she said sympathetically. "Thought you could use some water."

"Oh, thank you..." I said, taking the glass gratefully from her hand. "That was very kind of you."

I took a deep breath as she watched me with a slight smile on her face.

"You don't look like you're having a great time," she said, and I laughed a little.

"Oh, no it's fine, it's a wonderful event, and everyone's been so kind..."

She raised her eyebrow, and there was something so sympathetic about her look that I couldn't hold back a soft sigh.

"I guess I'm feeling a little out of my depth tonight. I don't know anyone..."

"Well, they do say it's not what you know, it's who you know. However, I'm sure that we can fix that for you...What's your name, hon?"

She wasn't that much older than me, but there was something comforting, almost sisterly about her tone.

"Gwen Love."

She brightened a little.

"Oh, I know Bobby and Marie Love from Connecticut! Lovely people. Marie and I put together a charity a few years back. Are you related to them?"

"I'm pretty sure I'm not," I said reluctantly. I wasn't quite sure how to tell this woman that most of my relatives were from small towns in Oklahoma rather than in any of the fashionable places she often ventured to.

"Ah, well, it's a big family, as I understand," she said with a shrug. "But I am just certain that I know you from somewhere..."

Before I could say anything, Donovan appeared at my side, grinning easily at the woman.

"Ah, Jordan. Good to see you again," he said. "Beautiful as ever."

She offered her hand for a squeeze, and her eyes, if anything, grew brighter and softer.

"Well, Donovan, I was wondering when you were going to pop up. I was just chatting with Gwen here..."

"And trying to get all of the dirt on me, I'm sure," he said with a chuckle. "How've you been, Jordan? I was sorry to hear about your divorce..."

They talked about a few things, moving from topic to topic with the easy grace of people who had known each other for years. Donovan kept me grounded with an arm around my waist; otherwise I might have drifted back off into the warm Atlanta night. When Jordan spotted someone else she wanted to speak to, Donovan turned to me with a wry grin.

"Still got all your fingers and toes?"

"Um, what?"

"Jordan DuPleiss. She's got teeth, and she knows how to use 'em."

"I thought you liked her," I said in surprise.

"Oh, I do, but even her best friends aren't going to deny that the woman's a shark. She's been meaner since her divorce. I hope she didn't try to take a bite out of you."

"She was perfectly nice," I protested. "I am still glad that you came over, though."

Donovan's eyes softened as he looked at me, and his hand came up to cup the back of my neck.

"You look like you might be okay heading in for the night...."

I wavered. If I could do a ten hour shift on my feet at the restaurant, there was no reason that I couldn't finish out the evening at a party, but Donovan was right. I felt like someone who was struggling to keep my head above water, and with every moment that went past, I was sinking a little deeper.

"I don't want to make you miss anything..."

Donovan stepped a little closer, looking straight into my eyes. There was a strength and a command in his gaze that made my heart beat faster and my mouth go dry.

"I'm not asking you to tell me what I want or need," Donovan said softly. "I'm asking you to tell me if you're done, and you want to head back to the house."

I swallowed hard.

"Yes," I said in a small voice. "I'd like to be somewhere quiet with you now. Please."

Even though I was making him leave his part early, a slight smile came across his face, and he leaned down to give me a gentle kiss that made me melt into him.

"Of course," he said, and he took my hand in his.

8

CHAPTER EIGHT

Donovan

Gwen was quiet on the way back to the house, her small hand resting on my thigh the whole way back. When I glanced at her during the drive, she looked dreamlike, far away. A part of me relished the quiet. So many women who had sat where she was now had filled the air with words, trying to land a hook in me that would take. Another part of me wanted her to speak again. She wasn't loud, but silence felt like a strange garment on her.

When we were inside, I turned her to me with a slight smile, brushing a lock of hair out of her eyes.

"Do you need to sleep right now?" I asked softly. There was a worn look in her eyes, as if the evening had taken more out of her than she expected, but to my surprise, she shook her head firmly.

"I don't need to sleep right now," she said. "I want to give you your present."

I raised my eyebrow, tilting my head at her. She frowned.

"You did say that I could get you something...."

"I did. I guess I'm surprised you remembered," I admitted.

She smiled a little at that.

"Well, I couldn't find anything to buy you. I guess all those magazine articles were right, and buying gifts for the man who has everything is more difficult than I thought it would be. But I do have a present for you. Would you sit down in that chair, please?"

I sat down in the armchair she indicated, and watched in fascination as she fussed around the living room. First she removed her shawl, revealing her bare arms and her curves in that gorgeous dress, and then she stood just a few feet in front of me, her eyes on the ground.

For a single irresistibly hot moment, I thought she was going to strip, and then, she started to sing.

"I have wandered far, seeking the only star I ever knew..."

Her voice was almost piercingly sweet, perfectly controlled and lovely. I had heard it before, of course, but this was different. There was a quality in her voice that could have moved a stone to tears, and I felt frozen as I listened to her. I couldn't take my eyes away from her if I wanted to, and it almost felt as if my heart had gone hot and still in my chest.

Though it felt that she sang with all of her heart, Gwen kept her eyes on the floor, and even as her melody wove around us, I found myself wanting more than anything to see her eyes.

Look at me, look at me, I thought. I needed to see her. She was within reach, but there was something almost profane about touching her when she was in this state. It would feel like taking a masterpiece painting and smashing it on the ground.

Instead, I listened, hearing her words about a bird that led a girl to her love, and all of the difficulties she had to face while searching for him. In the end, they fell into each other's arms, and at that moment, Gwen looked up at me, her eyes glowing as the song subsided on the last note and she fell silent.

The silence stretched between us, and she clasped her hands lightly in front of her, as if she were nervous.

"Well, I hope you liked it," she said, searching my face for some sign of approval. "I've been working on it for a while, but, well... I guess it didn't come together until just today."

"So I was the first one to hear it?"

I got up and crossed the floor to stand in front of Gwen. She looked away, but I touched her chin, making her look up again.

"Gwen?"

"You were," she said, her voice shaking just a little. "I... I wanted you to be the first one to hear it. It was for you. In every way that matters."

She was shivering a little, and then there was nothing in the world that could have kept me from taking her in my arms.

"It was the best present anyone has ever given me," I rasped, drawing her closer to me. "I loved it." *Love* was not a word that ever fell lightly from my lips, and the awareness lingered that I might love far more than her beautiful gift, though I didn't allow myself to dwell on it.

Having her small soft form pressed against me was enough to send a shiver of need through my body, and I lifted her in my arms.

"I want you," I growled, kissing her throat. "I can't resist you..."

She sighed with pleasure as I kissed her, wrapping around me tightly.

"I don't just want you to," Gwen said quietly. "I need you."

Over the years, women have said the most extravagant things to me, trying to convince me of their devotion. Something about Gwen's quiet confession, soft, almost a whisper, tore right at my heart and made me hold her closer.

"Rare, precious beauty," I whispered, carrying her into the bedroom. Gwen breathed a soft sigh of pleasure when I laid her down on the bed. I hesitated a moment. I liked taking the lead, craved it most times, but what I wanted most right now was to please Gwen.

"Tell me what you want," I said, and smiled a little when it brought a flush of color to her cheeks.

"I don't know..." she murmured, and I tilted my head to one side.

"I think you do," I murmured silkily. "I think when I said that, something flashed in your mind. Why don't you tell me what that was, my darling?"

She swallowed, and I could hear the click of her dry throat.

"I want you to make love to me," she said.

Thoughtlessly, I laughed a little at her antiquated language. It was a little quaint, but perfect for her. There was a flash of hurt across her face, and to soothe her, I kissed her soft mouth gently, running my hands down her sleek sides until she was shivering with pleasure.

"Of course I will, darling," I murmured to her, and she clung to me, murmuring soft sweet words against me. She said something else, but I could barely make it out.

"What was that, sweetheart."

"I want you naked," she said, her voice more clear this time, and the heat that spilled through me was intense. It was intoxicating seeing her come into her own desire, learning more about what she wanted and asking me for it. I wanted to reward that particular kind of knowledge, and with a grin, I stood back from the bed, stripping off my clothes with deliberate motions. At first, I thought that she wouldn't be able to meet my eyes, let alone look at me, but her gaze as I shed my clothing was hungry, needy.

"You are very beautiful," she said, and I laughed again.

"Thank you," I purred. "May I take the same liberty?"

She started to unbutton her dress, but then I was there, undressing her tenderly. It was a gentle counterpoint to how I had stripped her the first time, and she sighed, pressing herself into my hands. In a few moments, she was as naked as I was. Gwen's hands came up to cover her breasts, but I tugged them back down.

"I never want you to cover yourself from me," I muttered, pressing hot kisses to her throat. "I always want to see you..."

She might have argued with that, but then my hand closed over her breasts, squeezing gently before I teased her nipple to hardness. She whimpered under her breath, and her breath caught as she reached between my own legs. She looked at me half-apprehensive, as if I would ever have pulled back from that.

"Here, shall I show you...?

I folded my hand over hers, stroking her palm along my erect shaft. I grew harder and fuller with every stroke, and I watched the way her eyes fluttered shut at the sensation of touching me and arousing me.

"Good girl, perfect girl," I ground out. Having her hand on me was intoxicating, and that was before she pulled back to swirl her thumb over the silky liquid at the very tip.

"I want you so much," she murmured, and with a groan, I reached down between her legs, spreading her open and cupping her sex briefly I ran my fingers along her slit. She parted easily for me, but when I pushed a finger inside her, she gasped a little.

"Tight?" I asked, and blushing again, she nodded. "Do you need to stop?"

Gwen' hesitated, and I touched her chin again, making her look at me. "Don't ever be afraid to be honest with me."

"I don't want to stop... but maybe I need it kind of slow?" Her request trailed off uncertainly, and I felt an unfamiliar pang of anger at who might have told her that she needed to be so hesitant with that information.

"Then of course we're going to be slow," I said with a smile. "After all, I've been thinking about this for a while."

Gwen started to ask what I meant by that, and then she whimpered as I shifted down her body, coming to rest on my belly between her legs. I opened her more fully with my hands, and when I ran the widest part of my tongue along her slit, she nearly came off of the bed in surprise and pleasure.

"Oh, Donovan!"

Her startled cry was nothing but sweetness to me, and I nuzzled between her legs, drinking in the intoxicating taste of her, wanting all of her. She groaned as I circled her clit with the tip of my tongue, and when I pressed my fingertip inside her opening again, her hands came down to tangle in my hair. Instead of pushing her away, however, I growled encouragingly, relishing in the display of her need.

I was startled by how little time it took to make her thighs start to shake, her heels drumming against the broad bed. Gwen's hands tightened almost painfully on my hair, but I refused to be pushed away, not when she was chanting *yes, yes yes* in a hushed and needy tone.

Her body arched like a bow, drawing tight for the flight of an arrow, and then with a deep groan that struck me low in the belly, she stiffened up with a cry. For one beautiful moment, every muscle in her body was tensed and then with a great cry, she relaxed again, falling down on the bed in a tangle of slender limbs. She was babbling something. Most of it was my name, and for a moment, I simply watched her. Her pleasure was beautiful, but I wasn't done yet.

She opened her eyes lazily when I came to lie down by her

side. She cried out in surprise when I pulled her astride my hips, looking up at her with a grin.

"Don't think that you're getting off so lightly..."

She shifted her weight I wrapped my hands around her hips, placing her just perfectly so that her wet warmth was positioned right above the tip of my cock. She whimpered at that intimate sensation, but the tension that strung through her body and the bright gleam in her eyes told me that she was as eager for what came next as I was.

We shifted together, and with my hands on her hips to guide her, Gwen pressed down on my cock, taking me fully in one slow, powerful stroke. She felt amazing wrapped around my cock like that, but I couldn't stand to simply enjoy that pleasure for now. The entire time I had been bringing her to pleasure, I had ached for her, and I didn't think I could wait much longer. My hands tightened on her hips, lifting her up and bringing her down on me again. She gasped with surprise at the motion, but then she was moving with, pushing our bodies together and making us both groan.

I had never felt anything as good, as right as Gwen. I had never known a woman as innocently intoxicating, as perfectly matched with my desire and my appetites. I couldn't help looking up at her as she rode me. There was something beautifully divine about her on top of me, giving me pleasure and taking it for herself as well.

The tension rose in me like the tide, and I gritted my teeth. I didn't want it to be over too soon, but I had put it off too long. With a muffled roar, I pushed into her, holding her hips hard to mine.

Gwen gasped, her nails digging into my chest, and when she felt me spill inside her, she sighed softly, going limp. I counted my breaths as she lay on top of me, listening in something like awe as we matched each other breath for breath.

"God, you're perfect," I murmured, but from the soft way she breathed on top of me, I didn't even think she had heard it. At last, I had to shift her off of me, pulling away with a faint regret.

"No, don't leave," Gwen murmured softly, reaching for me, and I shook my head.

"I'll be right back, darling," I promised. "I just want to take good care of you..."

I washed myself quickly in the bathroom, and then I came back with a small hand towel soaked in warm water.

"On your back,' I told her, and I smiled a little as she complied easily. She murmured in surprise as I pulled her legs apart again. It occurred to me that if I wanted her again, she would let me have her, as exhausted as she was, and that thought awakened another throb of desire in my body. I held it back, though, and instead I focused on cleaning her between the legs with the towel. She moaned with embarrassment at first, but then when she realized how very good it felt, she relaxed bed into the bed with a sigh.

"That feels so good," Gwen murmured, and I made a sound of assent.

"I always want to make you feel that way," I told her, and she offered me a bright and sleepy smile.

It was the truth, I realized. I wanted to make her feel good. I wanted to dress her in beautiful clothes and take them off of her, I wanted to make sure she had all of the time in the world to sing and to write her music, just so long as she would smile at me while she did it.

Before I was done, she had dropped off to a deep sleep. I crawled into the bed beside her, and as if we had slept together for years, she snuggled up next to me.

Can I keep her?

The dangerous thought wandered unbidden through my mind, though I had long ago dismissed the thought of getting married, and I pulled away from it now. I fell asleep to the idea of her traveling with me, of giving her an apartment that would delight her, all the while keeping her as close to me as I could.

CHAPTER NINE

Gwen

"Hey, watch it!"

I yelled, hanging on to the tall pile of dirty dishes with all of my might. Somehow, I managed to keep them from clattering to the ground, and the bus boy only shot me an aggrieved look as he hustled back to the kitchen. I started to go after him, but Andrea placed a gentle hand on my shoulder.

"Time for a break, babe," she said firmly. "We're out of the weeds now, and you're overdue."

I wanted to argue with her, but she was right. I dropped off the plates and followed her out to the courtyard to sit and to be out of the dining room for a moment.

"How long you been waiting tables?" she asked, and I shrugged.

"Since I was fifteen or so?"

"Yeah, that checks out. Point is, I've known you for years, and

I've never seen you come close to taking a spill as bad as the one that almost happened now. What's up? Is mystery man making you miserable?"

I blushed a little at that. Sometimes I wished I smoked just so I had something to do with my hands during awkward talks.

"I'm fine," I protested, but she shook her head.

"Hon, it looks to me like you got man problems. What's the real problem. He married or something?"

"No!' I said, offended, but Andrea shrugged.

"Figured it was worth asking. Can't think of too many reasons you might want to keep your man away from us. Carly was wondering if it was because he was an asshole, but I thought you were too smart for that. I was thinking maybe he was married."

"He's not," I said, looking down.

I hadn't been able to keep the fact that I was dating someone away from the sharp women I worked with, but I knew instinctively not to tell them about the.... arrangement that Donovan and I had somehow settled on.

"I care about you," he had bluntly informed me on the jet ride back to Florida. "Very much. But you should know what you are getting when you are with me."

I'd listened as he'd spoken of wanting to take care of me, to spend time with me. But then, he'd also cautioned me not to expect anything like marriage out of him. He'd informed me that if and when things ended, I was not to chase him! I had been so shocked by his blunt assessment of our relationship that I hadn't known what to say, and while I'd fumbled for the right words, he had taken my hand, squeezing it slightly.

"I'm not going to force you into anything, Gwen. I never will. But I want you. I care for you. I want to make you feel things that you haven't ever imagined before. But it needs to be your choice."

He had said that, and it had been on the tip of my tongue to tell him no, that I believed the songs I sang. I wanted love, passion and romance. Before I could, though, I had looked into his eyes, and seen a kind of vulnerability there that shocked me. His eyes were always so dark, but in that moment I'd noticed a kind of longing there that I'd previously missed.

Don't leave me.

There was more to Donovan than he let on, and in that single moment, I had decided to risk it all on my instincts.

"All right," I said. "I don't promise that I can do this, but... I want to try."

Donovan had looked immeasurably satisfied, and when he took my hand, there was something victorious about it.

"Good," he said. "You won't regret it."

As romantic declarations went, it wasn't what I had always dreamed of, but Donovan, in his own way, made up for it. He was mystified that I wanted to keep working; if he'd had his way, he would have kept me in one of the apartments he owned, or even in the penthouse itself. Instead, I insisted on working, and at night...

I still couldn't reconcile the passion that Donovan woke in me with the person I had been all my life. He took me to heights I had never dreamed of, and when I returned to the world, shaken by my own response, he held me close with the gentle kisses that I could barely believe came from the same man.

When I was with him, I felt safe and desired and cared for and perfect. Away from him... I didn't know what to think. I hadn't known until just now that it was getting obvious enough that my coworkers were keeping worried eyes on it, and I sat quietly for a moment before turning back to Andrea.

"I'm really fine," I said. "I guess I've just had a lot to think about..."

Andrea snorted, shaking her head.

"Sure, I'll believe that. You should bring him out sometime, see if he passes muster. If he doesn't, we'll send him packing."

I choked back a laugh thinking about Donovan coming out for drinks with the restaurant staff. I couldn't imagine that ending well, and I brought myself up short. He wasn't the one who had told me to keep our relationship a secret. He hadn't said anything of the sort. That was one demand he had not made. I had just done it on my own, and I suddenly felt more than a little strange.

There were dozens of reasons to keep our relationship quiet. Donovan owned the hotel. People might get jealous; they might start making all kinds of inferences about what I did or why I did it, and I didn't want that.

Had I done something wrong?

I was still thinking about that when I went to take the next round of orders. I wanted whatever it was that I had with Donovan to go well, but did I even know what a healthy relationship between the two of us might look like?

"Hi, I'm Gwen, and I'll be taking your order today, Can I get you started with some drinks?"

I said it dozens of times every day, but when I looked down at the woman who had just been seated, I felt the next words freeze in my mouth.

"Oh my god, Gwen," said Jordan. "What in the name of little green tomatoes are you doing here?"

Her words might have been kind, but her tone was positively delighted.

"I work here," I said stiffly. The last time I had seen this woman, I had been dressed in clothes that cost far more than my rent. Now I was in my usual drab restaurant uniform, and though I had never been ashamed of putting in a decent day's work before, I could feel an unpleasant heat prickling across my cheek.

"Oh, well isn't that delightful," she said, grinning and showing her teeth. "I was planning to get in touch with you after the gala, and for the life of me, I couldn't track you down. I guess I didn't think to look here... though perhaps I should have. I know that Donovan is in residence here somewhere, isn't he?"

"He is," I said automatically, and flinched a little when Jordan's smile got even wider. "But I, um, really should be speaking to you about the specials. I'm on the job."

If anything, Jordan's smile got wider. She leaned forward in her chair a little, and all I could think about was a big cat getting ready to strike.

"Oh I don't think you need to worry about that right this moment, do you? We're just having a little chat, I'm sure the manager won't mind."

I fiddled uncertainly with my pad and pencil, and Jordan looked me over. I could tell that she was taking in all of it, the uniform, the lank hair, the slight sheen of sweat from having been on my feet all day.

"My, my, I had no idea that Donovan was picking up friends at work. And here I thought you were from up the coast. You know, someone important."

I would never have called myself important at all, but when I heard her dismissal, it stung.

"Well, you certainly did fool a lot of people," she purred. "There was more than one gentleman there who didn't know you were with Donovan Fox and was interested in an introduction. Won't they be surprised."

She paused like a cat relishing playing with a mouse.

"And Donovan, my goodness. I thought he knew better than to play with the help."

I'd had enough, but it wasn't for the reasons that Jordan thought. I spun on my heel and dashed back to the kitchen, and all the way back, I wasn't thinking of Jordan at all. Instead, I thought of Donovan and the feelings I had for him. I wasn't the things that Jordan implied I was... but then I realized that for all rights and purposes, I was. I was the girl who worked the restaurant rush. I was something that Donovan was playing with, no matter how kind he was being about it. It was true, and Jordan was just the straw that broke the camel's back. This needed to end.

"Gwen, what the hell... Are you all right?"

Something about the desperate look on my face told Gus not to argue when I hurried for the lockers.

"I'm done, I need to be gone," I said.

"Gone? As in—Are you quitting?" he asked in disbelief.

"Yes... no..." I shook my head, knowing that such a wishy-washy response was not going to do me any favors. "I just need to be gone. Just... Gone."

I stayed in the locker room until I had stopped shaking, and I suppose I must have looked terrible because no one bothered me. Instead, they let me sit for an hour or more, and then finally, I was able to change into street clothes and pack my bag to leave. I crossed the atrium on my way out, and with a panicked pang, I saw Donovan and Jordan talking and laughing at the entrance. Donovan had some papers in his hand, but he looked down at Jordan with amusement and affection. Jordan looked positively coquettish as she tilted her face up towards him, and as I watched she touched the buttons on his shirt lightly with her fingertips.

That's what Donovan's real match looks like, whispered a small voice in my mind. *That's what he needs.*

I swallowed hard trying to keep myself from falling to pieces, and then I was gone. Just gone.

CHAPTER TEN

Donovan

Gwen had turned her phone off that afternoon. She never did that, and it bewildered me. When I called the restaurant, they told me with some asperity that she had left far earlier than she should have. I felt a strange prickle up the back of my neck, but refused to pay it any attention. Of course Gwen was fine. I refused to believe she could be anything else.

Then she didn't show up for our dinner date that evening and an unnerving, unfamiliar fear ran down my spine. I called her again, but her phone was off, and in desperation, I tracked down her address online and drove over to her place, thinking about all of the reasonable things I wanted to say, however angry and worried she had made me.

Then when she opened the door, red-eyed and dressed in plain shorts and a baggy T-shirt, I forgot all of them.

"I don't care to be stood up," I said, staring down at her, but she only shook her head dully.

"I can't do this any more," she said softly. "I'm sorry. I can't. I'm not what you want me to be, and I'm definitely not what people think I am."

"What are you talking about?" I demanded. I reached forward to touch her, but she drew away. I felt a hot pang go through me, and I bit down on it hard.

"I'm saying that it's over, I think," she said in a small voice. "I can't keep doing this. This is... you're right. It's not romance. It's something else and I can't do it."

"You agreed to this," I said, my voice thudding like a hammer. "We've been doing it for nearly a month now..."

"And now it's over," she said with a tired shrug. "It's time I get back to my life and you get back to yours, to the hotel, to Jordan. You said you would never force me, and so now that I want out... you have to respect that. You ... don't get to chase me either, Donovan."

Hearing my words thrown back in my face, however gently, was like a bucket of ice water.

For a moment, I wanted to snarl at her. To hell with that. No one told me what I had to respect, what I had to bow to. Not when I wanted Gwen like fire, not when something in me cried for her as the one source of pure goodness and truth and beauty in my world.

"Gwen..."

"No..." she said, her voice cracking. "I can't do this. I won't do this. You said this wasn't romance or a proper relationship. So it's not a breakup. It's just an end, Donovan. You need to leave."

I opened my mouth to argue with her again, but then she looked up at me, wide eyed and desperate. That was when I knew that I could never do anything that would bring her pain. There was so much pain in her gaze that it broke my heart.

"Sweetheart..."

"This isn't..." her voice cracked and her eyes, already so red from crying, gleamed once again with unshed tears. "This isn't something where you can give me orders," she said softly. "This is... real life. We had some kind of wonderful fantasy, but it's over now. I'm done. I have to be."

What else was there for me to say? I stood back. I reached for her, wanting to touch her face one last time, but I stopped myself. She watched me with those beautiful eyes, and I wondered if she was afraid I could talk her into coming back with me. I cleared my throat, my voice gone unexpectedly rusty.

"Goodbye, Gwen."

I walked down the long musty hallway of her apartment, listening for the click of the door as she closed it after me. It never came, and instead I could feel her gaze on my back until I turned the corner.

IN A HAZE, I drove back to the hotel and found myself in the penthouse because where the hell else was I going to go? The place was exactly the same as it had been a few hours ago, when I had been blithely expecting Gwen to return, but as the sun set, giving the room long and searching shadows, it took on a haunted quality.

I was being ridiculous and I knew it. I stalked to the bar where I poured myself two fingers of whiskey into a cut-glass tumbler. The strong smoky burn returned me to myself, but maybe that was the moment where I realized I didn't really like that self all that much.

There was a small mirror set behind the bar, and when I glanced at myself in it, I felt a wave of anger and disgust well up in me. I pitched the glass at the mirror with all my strength. The shattering sound was felt not good, but right. It felt so good that

I reached for another glass and after throwing down another few fingers of whiskey, I did it again.

I WOKE up the next morning with a pounding head, sprawled on the couch and surrounded by the wreckage of my own idiocy. The pale light coming in the window told me that it was barely past dawn, but there was no way I could get back to sleep, no matter how appealing unconsciousness felt right now.

All that mattered to me was that Gwen was gone, and she wasn't coming back. Somehow, I had pushed her away, and then I had let her simply go without fighting. I let the intense pain of that roar up inside me, felt all its hot edges and its terrifying fury, and when it subsided to a slightly more functional level, I finally breathed.

Gwen was something special, and though I could physically live without her, it would be hell and there would likely not be much left of me at the end of it. Gwen made me better, in every possible way. I was kinder around her, more honest, more appreciative of the beauty of a world that all my money sometimes occluded. Though I admittedly hadn't been very kind with that airplane speech. The memory made my gut clench and the alcohol still flooding my veins roiled in warning.

As I fought the nausea, a memory tugged at my mind. During that terrible encounter at her little apartment, she had mentioned Jordan. Why the hell would she mention Jordan? Jordan was staying at the hotel, I knew, but she hadn't mentioned running into Gwen.

I felt something like ice reach inside my chest and freeze hard. It helped. It gave me a place to put away the rage and the heat and the fear. I showered using that perfect cold to keep me going. I shaved, dressed in new clothes, and called down to housekeeping to let them know there was a serious mess in the penthouse. Honestly, I was more of a mess than anything I'd destroyed last night, but they couldn't help me. Only one person could.

I knew that this cold couldn't last long. If it did, it might last forever, and I got a vivid idea of what life might be like without Gwen.

Finally, I took a deep breath, and reached for my phone.

"Why, Donovan," Jordan purred, her voice low and sensuous. There was a time when it would have at least piqued my interest, but now it only infuriated me.

"I need to talk to you," I growled. "I'm coming down to your room."

A pause.

"Well, that's a lovely surprise."

"Shut up." I said. "I want answers."

11

CHAPTER ELEVEN

Gwen

Carly got me the waitressing job across town. It wasn't as nice as the job at the hotel, and frankly the owner gave me the creeps, but at the end of the day, it was work, and I needed it. I wasn't going back to Fox Hotel and Suites, not for any amount of money. Gus begged, something I never thought I'd see, but I was unwilling to take the chance of running into Donovan and Jordan, arm in arm, laughing together.

Though I wanted Donovan to be happy, I knew what I could tolerate and seeing that was something I considered a physical impossibility. I'd lose it.

I had ended things with Donovan almost two weeks ago, but though my mind knew it, my body and my heart weren't playing along. My body still tingled sometimes where he had touched me. My heart still leaped whenever I saw a man who was his size and with his hair color. I was a mess, and I couldn't even say that

I had learned my lesson. Somewhere underneath it all, I would have gone back if he had been willing to ask for me, to fight for me.

But of course, he wouldn't. No chasing.

With my roommate out of town for a conference, I spent my work day dreaming about getting home, kicking off my shoes, and trying to find my way back to the music which had temporarily gone to sleep inside me.

At least that's what I thought I was going to do before I walked up to the building and found Donovan seated on the front steps, waiting for me. His eyes were closed, his face tilted up to catch the last rays of the setting sun, and for one shocked moment, I simply took in the dark circles under his eyes, the hard set of his jaw. Then Donovan opened his eyes and looked at me, and there was such a depth of pain in his gaze that I nearly cried out.

"Gwen..." he said, and in a moment, he was on his feet, throwing his arms around me in an embrace that felt almost desperate.

I stood stiffly, not daring to let down my guard. "Donovan, what are you doing here?"

"I came for you," he said, pulling back just a little. "Gwen, I need you."

God, how many times had I imagined him coming to me and saying just that, but I couldn't do it. Not when his kind of need would eventually kill me with its indifference.

"Donovan, I can't do this again," I whispered, stepping back. "I'm sorry. Please go."

Donovan looked devastated for a moment, but then a fierce look came over his face, dark and possessive. When I tried to draw back, one hand fell on my shoulder and the other cupped my face, bringing my gaze up to his again.

"No. Not until you've heard what I have to say. Then I'll leave.

I'll never see you again if that's what you want, but you need to hear me now."

I nodded, unable to talk for the lump in my throat. When he saw that I was going to listen, Donovan took a deep breath.

"I need you in my life," he said, his voice urgent. "When you left, I felt as if I had been set at sea on a boat with no sail and no rudder. It was empty without you, and the emptiness felt like it was going to reach up and devour me."

He so closely described the emotions that I had been feeling all month that I gasped. Once I had tried to sit down and to write it into a song, but it had only made me cry.

"Donovan..."

"Let me finish, please. Then... I suppose you can do as you see fit. I can't stop you, and if you think you would be happier without me, I suppose I will find a way to live with it.

"But...Gwen... do you really want to? We were good, so good together. You made me feel like no one ever has before. I nearly killed Jordan when I realized she had said that shit to you. You belong with me. I... I can change. I want to change, because it's you. You are the only woman that I have ever, ever had these feelings for.

"Gwen, I need you. Not just your voice or your body. All of you. Your heart. Your eyes. Your smile. Your shy, sweet beauty. God, Gwen. I love you. Please."

The look on his face was haunted as he said words I was sure he'd never before said to anybody. And yet ...

I swallowed hard. I wanted to say yes, to fall into his arms and to let him take care of everything again. I couldn't though. Not with a man who didn't know me well enough to know what I wanted, a man who could turn away and just let me leave.

"I can't... "I said, and I started to walk away blindly.

From behind me, I could more feel than hear Donovan draw in his breath, and then, amazingly, he started to sing. His voice was low and cracked slightly. It was a good voice, but untrained, and the song had been written for my soprano.

"She fell in love, down a deep deep well, and there was no one to tell her no..."

I turned around in disbelief, and Donovan kept on singing, his voice breaking more than it had before. It was my song, the song I had sung to him once. He sang about love as I saw it, as I needed it to be, and with a choked cry, I spun around and threw myself into his arms.

"Thank God," he muttered raggedly, holding me so tight I could barely breathe, and I didn't want to. I never wanted to breathe again without his arms around me. Tilting my chin up, he kissed my lips, then my eyes, my nose, my forehead, whispering, "God, I love you, I love you, Gwen. I'm so sorry. Please don't ever leave me."

I looked up into his eyes, swept away by the depths of the truth in them. "I love you too, Donovan. So much. But it has to be different this time. I already love you. You don't need to buy me."

He kissed me again, threading his fingers through my hair and rubbing the ball of his thumb gently over the curve of my cheek. "It will be. Because so help me, Gwen, if you walk out again, I'll chase you next time. And you damn well better come after me if I do anything stupid."

His eyes gleamed and I smiled into them, leaning up into his hungry, passionate kiss as he lifted me into his powerful arms. "Deal."

©Copyright 2020 by Michelle Love - All rights Reserved
In no way is it legal to reproduce, duplicate, or transmit any part of this document in either electronic means or in printed format. Recording of this publication is strictly prohibited and any storage of this document is not allowed unless with written permission from the publisher. All rights are reserved.
Respective authors own all copyrights not held by the publisher.

❀ Created with Vellum

www.ingramcontent.com/pod-product-compliance
Lightning Source LLC
LaVergne TN
LVHW011738060526
838200LV00051B/3231